*Jan Caswell*

# hand artists

Designed by Bhairavi Patel

ISBN 978-1-937650-25-4
Library of Congress Control Number: 2013940212

SMALL
BATCH
BOOKS

493 South Pleasant Street
Amherst, Massachusetts 01002
413.230.3943
smallbatchbooks.com

# hand artists

### did you
## see
### what they
## said
?

by

**jan caswell**

illustrations by

**stephanie labrie**

# A note from the author and the illustrator

It is almost impossible to translate signs from American Sign Language (ASL), a dynamic and three-dimensional language of movements, to the static and two-dimensional printed page. Signs are spoken with hands, body language, and facial expression. Through gestures, motion, and passion they convey concepts, activity, and emotion. Showing the ASL movements and feelings accurately with line drawings and written descriptions is a huge challenge, and one that will never be as visually potent as signing in real life.

In some cases, you'll see that, for the sake of simplicity, we have taken artistic license in depicting certain signs. For example, because signed numbers often involve unique hand motions that cannot be shown in two dimensions, we have shown our page number signs as individual numerals—i.e., page 12 uses the signs for 1 and 2. We've also employed the use of arrows to indicate motion and direction of hands and arms when making certain signs. HAND ARTISTS is not meant to teach American Sign Language; instead it is an introduction to a different method of communicating. We hope you enjoy the experience!

**—J. C. and S. L.**

**HAND ARTISTS: DID YOU SEE WHAT THEY SAID?** was written to honor the Deaf community, whom I have had the pleasure of working with my entire professional life. Not only did they teach me their beautifully expressive sign language, they also welcomed me into their culture. I am forever grateful for the gifts of their hands and hearts!

I also want to thank my wonderful, amazing family—Mom and Dad (the Barbers); my children (Ben and Erin), and my life partner (Ferna)—for their unconditional love, patience, and support throughout our lives together. Words alone cannot express my feelings for each of you; I hope my actions do.

—Jan Caswell

**My journey through life** has been inspired by so many amazing people who have all contributed to this book in some manner. I can't thank you all enough for the love and support.

Losing my hearing hasn't been a disability, rather an enhancement of my other abilities. It's been a beautiful journey—and all I can say is don't stop believing!

—Stephanie Labrie

HAND ARTISTS was made possible through Kickstarter, a crowd fundraiser, with the support of more than one hundred generous people, without whom this project of love would not have happened. To each of you, a sincere, heartfelt thank you.

A special note of gratitude to the following contributors: Eric Dufour; Joanne Labrie; Lions Club of Southampton, Massachusetts; Quota Club of Holyoke, Massachusetts; and Andrew Sawyer.

**THEATER**

BARBER BARBER
WELCOME · KYLEIGH

**i** love going to Erin's house. It's like going to a private theater, with a new "movie" to watch each time I visit. Erin's family is so expressive— they talk to each other with their hands. I ring the doorbell and see the lights flash to alert Erin and her family that someone is at the front door.

**E**rin's mom comes to the door, wiping her
hands on her apron, then gives me a thumbs-up
for my goal in the soccer game. (I sign "thanks.")
She points upstairs, but I can already hear the
boom-boom of Erin's music playing in her room.

**i** bound up the stairs, bang on the door adorned with her favorite saying ("I'm NOT Deaf; I'm Ignoring You"), and barge in. Erin looks up from her book and wiggles her fingers hello. I salute in return.

I'm NOT
Deaf;
I'm Ignoring
You

**DEAF**
Move index finger
from mouth to ear.

**h**olding her palms up, she gives me a puzzled look and raises her eyebrows to ask, "What do you want to do?" I respond by pretending to play video games. Erin jumps off her bed and we grab chairs in front of her computer.

**L**ater, Mrs. Barber comes into the room and flashes the lights to get our attention. Mrs. B motions like she's eating, points at me, then at the floor. I nod my head up and down vigorously, gladly accepting her dinner invitation.

**d**inner at Erin's house rocks (and I can smell the chicken potpie).

 make a "hang ten" hand near my ear, signaling that I need to phone my mom for permission. Mrs. B signs "OK."

**d**ownstairs, Erin helps me use the video-phone to call my house. She types in a code, a face and hands appear on the screen, and Erin's flying fingers tell the interpreter my phone number. Soon the woman signs back, "The phone has been answered." Erin quickly asks Mrs. D (that's what she calls my mom), "Can Kyleigh eat dinner here?"

**m**y mom's response, on the interpreter's hands, is typical. "Oh, your mom must be making her famous chicken potpie, huh?"

**e**rin says, "Good guess, Mrs. D!"

My mom gets in the last word. "But no sleepover tonight—you girls have a soccer game tomorrow." Erin fingerspells fast, "OK, TTFN" (ta-ta for now . . . bye-bye).

**k**itchens can be noisy places, but you'd think when everyone talks with their hands, it might be quiet. NOT! Erin's big brother, Ben, and her dad are rehashing last night's hockey game, play by play by play.

**b**en scored a hat trick (three goals in one game), and Mr. Barber threw his favorite baseball cap on the ice. That's a tradition that means congratulations.

**W**atching their hands dart, jerk, and shoot the puck over the table, just barely missing the glasses of milk, we can see every pass, slap shot, and score again!

**m**rs. B bangs the stove with her ladle to get our attention and we grab our plates to be served from the steaming potpie. We all sit down and dig into our food.

**t**he lights flash again, signaling a phone call. Mr. Barber teases Ben that it must be his girl-friend, but since the videophone will take a message, no one jumps up to answer it.

## FRIEND
Hook left index finger around right index finger, then reverse.

Mr. Barber
American
Sign Language
101

**M**r. Barber gets everyone's attention by pounding on the table with his knuckles so we can feel the vibrations. He puts his glasses on the end of his nose, then claps his hands together twice. Uh-oh . . . that means school . . . for me.

**m**ealtime is my sign language lesson at the Barbers. They tell jokes to teach me their language . . . and I sure do make them laugh with my efforts to read their signs. I learn about twenty-five new signs each time and forget half of them before the next lesson.

### SCHOOL
Clap hands together two times.

### LIBRARY
Form "L" with index finger and thumb and make a circle counterclockwise.

### BOOK
Mime opening a book with palms together, then open thumbs out.

### WRITE
Mime writing on paper. With right thumb and index finger together, make a scribbling motion on left palm.

### PAPER
With a sliding, upward movement, tap right hand, palm down, against left palm twice.

**t**onight's spelling test (to help me read finger-spelling better) is on sports-related terms from Ben's hockey game and from Erin's and my soccer game.

G O A L

**Y**ou try reading "penalty kick," "hat trick," "offsides," "slap shot," and "goal" on Mr. Barber's fingers. It's tough . . . and he does not slow down for me.

PENALTY KICK

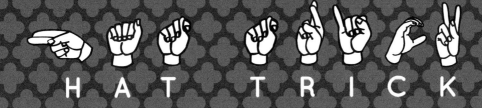

HAT TRICK

OFFSIDES

# FAMILY

## FAMILY
Form "F" with each hand by pinching thumb and index finger together and extending other fingers. Then, starting with pinched fingertips touching, palms facing, rotate hands until pinkies touch.

## MOTHER
With outspread fingers perpendicular to face, tap thumb against chin twice.

## FATHER
With outspread fingers perpendicular to face, tap thumb against forehead twice.

## SISTER
With fist, touch extended thumb down side of cheek, then extend index fingers and tap together.

## BROTHER
Mime grabbing the brim of a cap, then extend thumbs and index fingers and tap one fist over the other.

## GRAND-MOTHER
Begin by forming "mother" sign, then move hand away from chin.

## GRAND-FATHER
Begin by forming "father" sign, then move hand away from forehead.

**W**e all laugh together at my attempts to sign with the Barber family. Each of us has our own individual sign name, so we know who we're talking about.

Mr. Barber's sign name is "Haircut," of course.

Mrs. B is the letter "B" on her heart.

Erin is the letter "E" near her mouth because she smiles (and talks) a lot!

Her brother is cute so I have my own sign for him: I form a "B" and touch my chin to signify "cute." Everyone else uses "BB," his initials, near the forehead.

**i** am learning to fingerspell, but it's easier to express myself with my hands, slowly, than to read their fast fingerspelling. When they sign, they draw stories in the air.

If I pay close attention, I can follow the pictures they paint with their hands. Each of the Barbers has his or her own style of hand art.

**SKY**
With one forearm on the other (like a genie), move top arm up at right angle toward the sky.

**STORY**
With open hands, bring thumbs and index fingers together and pull apart as if you're stretching something. Repeat.

**m**rs. B paints softly, like a watercolor with flowing lines. Mr. Barber's hand art style is more like painting with thick, heavy strokes and bold colors. Ben has his own crazy way of stabbing at the air, kind of like graffiti you see in the city: colorful and quick. Most of his sign language "paintings" make me laugh, because he is always teasing me.

**m**y buddy Erin draws with an eye for detail. She uses her hands to gently paint in all the shading and color combinations so that I understand exactly what she means. To talk to Erin, I gesture as clearly as I can. We communicate just fine most of the time.

 **m**y art looks like stick figures, by the way!

 lthough she can speak pretty well, Erin doesn't need to use her voice with me. When one of us looks puzzled, we use fingerspelling to clear up the confusion.

**m**any signs mimic actions; for instance, driving a car, playing baseball, holding a baby.

## DRIVING A CAR
Mime driving a car, with hands on steering wheel turning left and right.

## PLAYING BASEBALL
Mime swinging a bat.

## HOLDING A BABY
Mime cradling a baby in your arms.

**O**ther signs are much harder to figure out, but they make sense when they're explained; for instance, "understand." You hold your fist near your forehead, then snap your index finger into the air—like a light bulb going on in your head, because you got it!

**Y**es and no are really easy. Yes: Curl your fist up and down (like you're knocking). No: Tap your first two fingers against your thumb of the same hand. Shake your head yes or no for emphasis.

YES

NO

 **if you don't understand, you can just shrug your shoulders—everyone understands that.**

**e**rin and I spend lots of time talking about soccer, school, boys, clothes, what we want to be when we grow up, and music. (She LOVES music, LOUD MUSIC, so she can feel the vibrations.)

## DOCTOR
With index finger extended, and other fingers bent, tap twice on the opposite up-turned wrist.

## DREAM
Touch extended index finger to forehead, then move hand out while curling finger up and down.

## SOCCER
Swing open right hand to "kick" the closed left hand.

**W**hen Erin signs to me, her language really comes alive. Her hands are always in motion, and her face emphasizes what she is saying.

FUNNY

WHO

HAPPY

WHAT

SAD

WHERE

MAD

WHEN

**e**rin's facial expressions crack me up, but they also really help me understand her. I never knew you could say "NO" in so many ways!

## INTERPRETER

With index and thumb fingertips of each hand touching in front of the chest, palms facing each other, twist hands in opposite directions several times. Then move open hands down along sides of body (indicating a person).

In school Erin has a sign language interpreter, who signs what the teacher is saying so that Erin can understand the lessons. (Erin's really smart, especially in math and science.) Erin has good speech, so she can speak for herself and people understand her when she talks. But when it's just the two of us, it's more comfortable to turn off our voices.

 **e**rin's goal is to become a doctor when she grows up.

**i** want to play soccer professionally, but if that doesn't work out, maybe I'll teach deaf children.

**W**hen we're at soccer, I tell Erin what the coach is saying with signs. She doesn't wear her hearing aids during games or practice, so sometimes, when she doesn't hear the whistle blow, she speeds down the field all alone. Then she turns around, looks back . . . and starts laughing.

**d**uring games the refs and other teams don't know she is deaf and they wonder why she doesn't stop. Erin will point to her ears and shrug her shoulders, then she's back to the game. Her deafness doesn't hurt her soccer skills at all.

**e**rin is my best friend. We are alike in so many ways, and we have so much fun together. We share clothes and secrets, dreams and pizza, frustrations and successes.

She's taught me a new language and so much more. I guess the only big difference between us is that Erin is better at hand art than I am!

# PLACES IN A HOUSE

## HOUSE
Mime the shape of a house, with fingertips angled toward each other for the roof, then hands straight down for walls.

## TOILET
Form "T" with thumb between index and middle finger, make side-to-side shaking motion.

## KITCHEN
Form "K" (peace sign) with right hand, palm down on left palm, and flip hands over (like flipping a burger).

## LIVING ROOM
With "L" hands, move hands up from waist to shoulders. Then mime the four walls of a room by forming a box shape with parallel hands.

## BASEMENT
Move closed right fist in a circle under the left open hand.

## DINING ROOM
Pretend to eat with right hand. Then mime a box shape (for room).

## BEDROOM
Mime sleeping with one or both hands. Then mime a box shape (for room).

# SPORTS

### SOCCER
Swing open right hand to "kick" the closed left hand.

### BASKETBALL
Mime shooting a ball into a basket.

### TENNIS
Mime swinging a tennis racket (like a forehand shot).

### HOCKEY
Brush index finger of right hand against open palm of left hand (like a hockey stick sliding the puck).

### BASEBALL
Mime swinging a bat.

# MOVIE RELATED

## MOVIE/FILM
With heel of outstretched open right hand against side of perpendicular left hand, move right hand from side to side.

## MOVIE CAMERA
Mime holding an old-fashioned movie camera, with left hand holding camera and right closed hand moving in a circular motion beside it.

## THEATER
With both hands in fists, thumbs out toward chest, move hands in alternating upward circles.

## POPCORN
With fists facing up, alternate moving hands up and down while flicking out each index finger with a repeated movement (like kernels popping).

## TICKET
Use bent index and middle fingers of right hand like a ticket punch on side of open left hand.

# A-Z

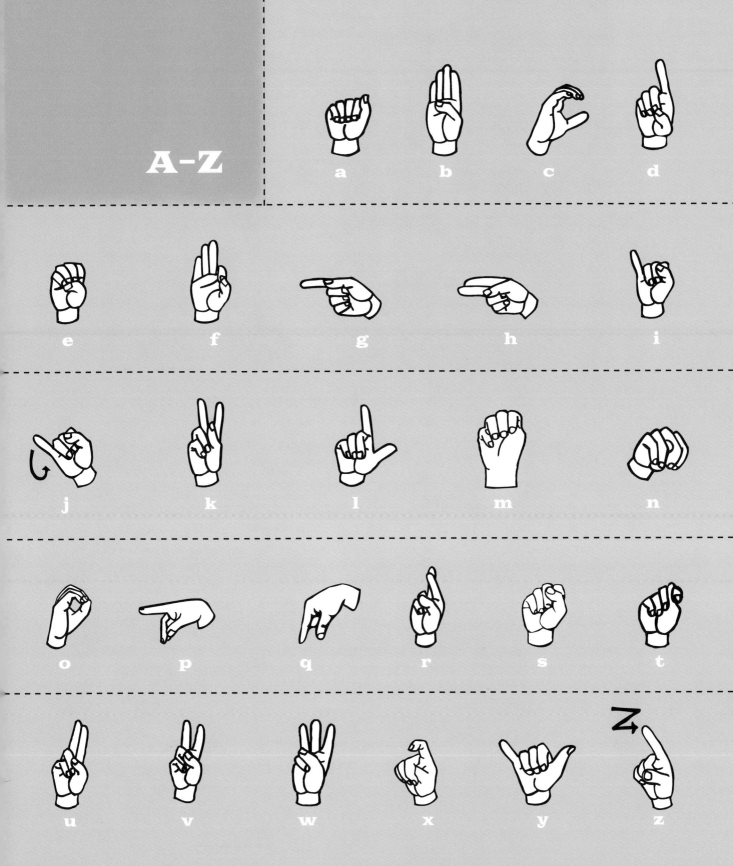

jan

**Jan Caswell** has loved American Sign Language (ASL) since she was introduced to it in her first job after college. Living with twenty-five teenage girls in a dorm at the Austine School for the Deaf, in Brattleboro, Vermont, she was fortunate to learn the language that would provide jobs throughout her career—from dormitory counselor to Vermont state coordinator of services for the Deaf to educational interpreter in California to vocational rehabilitation counselor for the Deaf in Massachusetts. Now retired from her state job, she is the founder and principal of Jan Caswell Associates, communication consultants serving deaf and hearing-impaired persons and the community around them.

In her spare time, Jan loves antiquing, repurposing "junk" for crafts, and serving on the boards of Austine School for the Deaf and Holyoke Community College Deaf Studies. She currently lives in western Massachusetts (though claims the Northeast Kingdom of Vermont as home) with her partner, Ferna, and their Australian Shepherd, Molly.

**Stephanie Labrie** is a multimedia artist, whose passion for art began at a very young age. Through the years her art has provided an outlet for dealing with certain life-changing events—most significantly, becoming a late-deafened adult due to the genetic disorder neurofibromatosis type II (NF2).

Stephanie took American Sign Language classes at Greenfield Community College, in Greenfield, Massachusetts, to aid her in the event of full deafness in the future. She later attended the Hartford Art School and focused her senior thesis on NF2 and ASL. Gradually, she's realized that her disability has actually heightened her other abilities. She would like to thank all of the amazing people who have helped contribute to this book, especially her mother, Joanne Labrie. This work is in memory of her father and sister.

CPSIA information can be obtained
at www.ICGtesting.com
Printed in the USA
BVIC011745240613
323921BV00004B

* 9 7 8 1 9 3 7 6 5 0 2 5 4 *